D0065362

BY THE SAME AUTHOR

Simple Spigott

illustrated by Jacqueline Tomes

A Borzoi Book for Young People
PUBLISHED BY ALFRED A. KNOPF

The Garret of Greta McGraw

Illustrated by
LESLIE GOLDSTEIN

The
GARRET
of
GRETA
McGRAW

Mary Francis Shura

ALFRED A. KNOPF : NEW YORK

1961

F
Shura

L.C. Catalog card number 61–7122

THIS IS A BORZOI BOOK,
PUBLISHED BY ALFRED A. KNOPF, INC.

Fourth Printing.

SA
3.90

In memory of DAN
and to
DANNY *of Shura 'Nuff Farm*

The Garret of Greta McGraw

1

Halfway up the stairs with her schoolbooks tight under her arm, Greta paused to listen. No doors were being opened or shut; there were no sounds of footsteps on the stairs or in the hall. A friendly silence filled the Trainor house.

Greta sighed with satisfaction. This hushed quiet made pretending seem almost real. As she took another deep breath she felt that everything about her was changing. It was as if her thick black hair suddenly became pale, floating to her shoulders in deep waves. Her dark eyes were now as blue as Mrs. Trainor's, and, instead of being "stick-thin" as Mother said, she was slender and tall and very grown-up, maybe seventeen even. Tucking in her tummy and squaring her shoulders as she did in gym class, Greta mounted the stairs.

"Blue dresses with long trains are very chic this year," she whispered to the imaginary friend sweeping along beside her.

"Indeed they are," the impressed friend whispered back. "And yours is so lovely."

While Greta was nodding her head graciously, she was startled from her game by a loud apple-biting noise that seemed almost in her ear.

It was her neighbor Peter, smiling as he leaned against the newel post on the landing just above her. No, he was not smiling, Greta thought unhappily; he was sneering because he had caught her in her make-believe world.

"Why don't you carry your books on your head?" he asked helpfully. "It might help hold your chin down, Gertie."

"Greta," she corrected coldly, brushing past him to mount the next flight of stairs.

"Gertie is a silly goat, went and dropped her petticoat." Peter made a ridiculous chant of the words. Greta turned to stare at him angrily. She simply could not stand Peter when he acted like this. There was no point in denying the part about the petti-

coats, either, since he had obviously already heard about her mishap. Mother had been so upset when she left for work that she must have told Peter's mother about it on the way to the bus stop. Of course Peter *would* listen.

Not that Greta blamed Mother for being angry,

although it was an accident. She had been putting her sweater box away when she knocked the petticoats down. The whole hanger gave way and fell. They caught the edge of the toybox, spilling old blocks and doll furniture and worn-out crayon pieces all over the floor.

"You cannot play with Peter or do anything that's fun until this closet is cleaned up perfectly," Mother had said, glaring at the dreadful mess spilling out into the room.

"Gertie is a silly goat," Peter chanted again, grinning happily at Greta.

"I'll have you know, Peter Knowles," she said firmly, "I have more important things to do than listen to you."

"There's nothing more important than picking up petticoats," he mocked her.

"That may be part of it," Greta ceded grandly. "But I also have a secret that can't be shared with rude people like you."

As Greta flounced on, she could feel Peter's stare following her. She had only added that last part because she knew that Peter could not stand anything secret. Unlocking the door with the key that she wore around her neck on a silver chain, Greta

let herself into the cool apartment. The rooms
smelled musty from being closed up all day.

As she flung open her bedroom window, she
sighed. She wished she had not told Peter that silly
old fib. She had no reason for doing it except that,
when Peter teased so rudely, she always wanted to
hit back in some way.

She leaned on her windowsill. From this view,
the house pointed itself at the street like a pale
brown finger. Two flights below on the fire escape
that had been added when the apartments were
put in, Miss Gray's yellow cat Caliph curled comfortably in the sun outside the window. He looked
up at Greta, yawning and stretching as if she had
been the cause of his awakening.

Suddenly Greta noticed that Caliph was not the
only one who was looking up. From the window
just below, a strange woman's face peered at her
curiously.

"I hate to bother you, dearie," the woman called
to her. "But I was halfway through a pudding when
I found myself short an egg."

Greta realized this must be the woman who had
put up polka-dotted curtains. Greta hesitated only
a minute before answering.

"I'm sure we have plenty. If you'd like one, I'll bring it down."

"I'll run up," the woman said cheerfully. "You're McGraw, aren't you?"

Greta waited inside the door, the egg cool and moist in her hand. The woman was shorter than Mother and heavier. The way her hair curled about her face would have given her a doll-pretty look if her eyes had not been sharp and searching.

"I'm Mrs. Owens," she introduced herself. "I'm not usually a borrower, but in the rush of moving in . . ." Her voice trailed off. She was looking past Greta into the McGraw apartment with such curiosity that it almost frightened Greta. The woman smiled quickly again. "Pardon me if I seem nosy," she said. "I just love these fine old houses and I'm always interested in how they're built."

"That's all right," Greta replied. She admitted to herself that she sometimes felt the same way about strange houses.

"You're top story, aren't you?" the woman asked. "Really the garret?"

"Garret?" Greta asked. This was a new word.

"Garret, attic, whatever you want to call it." The woman shrugged. "The place where the pitch of the eaves shows." She smiled again, but only with her mouth.

"I don't believe there is any attic here," Greta answered, quite confused by now. She felt that Mrs. Owens wanted to be invited in. Greta was sure that her mother would not approve of this. She handed Mrs. Owens the egg. "We're all there is to the top of the house, I'm sure."

"Back when Mrs. Trainor was a stage star, this was quite a place," Mrs. Owens commented.

Greta wished Mother had not made such a firm rule about not letting strangers into the apartment. Mrs. Owens obviously wanted to talk about the wonderful old days when Mrs. Trainor was young and beautiful and famous.

Greta loved listening to tales about those days. There had been no apartments here then. The house had been a great mansion where Mrs. Trainor, whose name was Morgan then, had lived with her sisters and her mother. They were all gay and young and beautiful. Greta had heard of the wonderful parties that they had held for their friends from the theater.

Mother had told her that even the neighborhood was different. Instead of Mr. Wong's Chinese laundry, the German bakery, and the other shops that lined the streets, there had been only fine houses.

When Greta said nothing, Mrs. Owens smiled at her again, taking a last, lingering look into the living room.

"You must come and borrow from me sometime," she said cordially. "If you like to read, we have loads of books. My husband's father was a writer . . ." She broke off suddenly, backing away from the door. "I'll return your egg."

Greta slipped the bolt quietly behind Mrs. Owens. The woman's curiosity had left her with an uncomfortable feeling.

Greta started picking things up from the floor of the closet to put back into the toybox. She made neat piles of doll furniture, game pieces and last year's weekly school news. The room seemed very quiet to her. Greta always thought of noises as being of two kinds, the near and the far. Right in the room there was a near kind of quiet with nothing but the tick of the old clock that Grandma Harris had sent Mother from the farmhouse in Vermont. From the street below came the far noises of car motors. Now and then a whistle or the blare of an auto horn would break the pattern.

A firm thump on the floor behind her startled Greta into shrieking with fright. A funny, weak, dizzy feeling made her sit very still with her dress pulled tight about her knees. She knew it was not the petticoats falling again because they were still draped across her bed. She had bolted the door behind Mrs. Owens, so she must be all alone. Her fright started a little sob down deep in her throat just as another sound began.

This was a low, rough, warm sound right in her ear. Greta's fear melted and she cried in relief as she turned to catch Caliph in her arms.

As she stroked the big yellow Persian, Caliph's back arched happily to her touch. "So you came in through that open window, you scamp," she said to him lovingly. "You scared me silly, you naughty old cat, you."

Caliph stayed to watch her work. He even played a little, slapping the piles of toys about. Once he wandered deep into the long narrow closet to look out at her. His large eyes glowed greenly yellow from the dimness at the far end.

By five-thirty Greta had smoothed the last hanger on the rack. She cocked her head to admire the way it looked. With the shelves so neat and the clothes sorted so carefully with each petticoat

on its private hanger, there should be no more
accidents.

Greta hurried to get the table set and her twenty
spelling words practiced before Mother got home.
She even remembered to unbolt the door. Mother's
return to the apartment was the nicest moment of
the whole evening. Greta did not want to spoil it
by having the door locked when she arrived.

It was always the same and this made it special
for Greta. Mother entered quickly, panting a little
from climbing the stairs. She always looked around
a moment before her face softened into a quick
smile for Greta. When she bent to kiss Greta's
face, her skin smelled clean and like the out of
doors. Somehow, the whole room seemed to stir
itself comfortably like a sleepy pup. Having
Mother there suddenly made it part of a home instead of a room at the top of a house.

"Come and see my closet before you start dinner," Greta urged, as her mother whisked an apron
from the peg by the door. "I worked very hard."

"That's wonderful, dear," Mother said, tightening an arm around Greta's shoulders as she admired
it. "I'm sorry you had to stay in all alone, but we
must learn to be neat."

"Oh, I had company," Greta laughed. "The new lady downstairs, Mrs. Owens, came to borrow an egg, and Caliph came calling through my open window."

"Caliph," Mother repeated, her eyes widening. "That's funny. Miss Gray stopped me in the hall to ask if I had seen him. He wasn't waiting on the fire escape for her as usual, and she was concerned."

"He left here a little after five," Greta said calmly. "Maybe he was going to pay more calls before he went home."

But later, as Greta lay in her bed looking out sleepily at the stars dimmed by the glow of city lights, she heard something new among the far noises. It was the plaintive voice of Miss Gray calling, "Here Caliph, kitty, kitty, kitty" from below in the street.

"Surely he'll come back soon," Greta thought drowsily as she drifted off to sleep.

When she was awakened, it was so swiftly that she sat up blinking. Her heartbeat sounded loud in the quiet room. The sound that had startled her came again. Although it was loud and thumping, it seemed as close to her as a whispered word. The room was dark and far noises were hushed in the

middle of the night. Close to her again in the near quiet came the desperate thumping and scraping sound.

As Greta listened, stiffened with fear, it seemed as if something that was trapped behind the wall of the room was struggling to get to her.

As she had told Mrs. Owens, there could not be an attic since this was the very top story. Yet the noise came again, making it hard for Greta to breathe easily. No matter how much she did not want it to be true, it seemed that something was trying to get to her right through the very walls of her room.

2

"I must be getting to be the worst kind of scaredy-cat," Greta told herself firmly. She shivered under her covers and listened to the urgent thumping sound coming again into her quiet room. "Silly old Caliph scared me coming in the window, and now this. But what can be making the noise?"

There were beautiful slate-and-white pigeons with ridgy pink feet that lived among the tops of the buildings in the neighborhood. But a pigeon would not be roof breaking at night. They always lined up on the ledge of the place next door and tucked their heads under their wings when the first colors of twilight came.

Mother would be sleeping soundly in the far room across the apartment. Greta fished on the floor for her slippers and pulled her pink bathrobe from the foot of the bed. That was what she must do, of course, waken Mother.

She had walked across the living room before she thought it over again. Mother hated the city so much and was so sure that they should move back to the village in Vermont where she had grown up. If this night noise frightened Mother too, it would be one more thing on the list of "Why children should grow up in the country," away from the clattery bustle of the city that Greta loved.

"I'll settle it my very own self," Greta said firmly. "It's only a skittery-scritch of a thumping noise anyway, not anything terrible."

Since the sound seemed to be coming from the outside, Greta opened her window as far as it would go. From the darkness of her own room, the outside world seemed to be flooded with pale lights that melted into the deep shadows of the surrounding buildings. The fire escape curled like lace in the night, and the street lights stood in little puddles that looked like leftover daylight. Leaning out very carefully, Greta searched the walls of the Trainor house with her eyes.

The pigeons cooed a little, stirring on the ledge across the way, but there was nothing else moving. The tiny square of light down near the street level would be Mrs. Trainor's window. Greta realized unhappily that Miss Gray also must be still awake, waiting fearfully for Caliph's safe return.

Greta was still hanging out looking about when the noise came again, sharper this time and so near her that she gasped.

"The wall," Greta whispered aloud to herself. "It has to be something in the wall, or the closet."

Greta found the flashlight that Mother kept in the drawer of the kitchen cabinet. Aiming the beam of light very carefully, she searched every inch of the shelves and floor and wall of the closet. Even after she was convinced that there was nothing there, the sound persisted.

Greta was almost ready to give up and call Mother when the beam of the flashlight cast the shadow of something she had not noticed before. It was a round knob, forcing its way through the wallpaper of the closet. It was like the knobs on the art cabinets at school. Greta pulled her bathrobe tighter and went to the far end of the closet to in-

vestigate. Very carefully, for she knew that tearing wallpaper was not a good thing to do, she loosened the pale blue covering about the knob. Soon the whole latch was showing in the flashlight's gleam.

But why a latch in the back of her closet? Feeling very reckless, and spurred on by the noise now sounding even louder from behind the closet wall, Greta pulled the whole strip of wallpaper off and found a little door. It was crusty from the dried paste where the wallpaper had been glued over it, and the latch was very hard to work, but she finally jiggled it free.

As the door came ajar, a rush of cold air struck Greta and a firm body brushed against her. Warm and furry and purring with welcome, Caliph greeted her with happy gratitude for his release.

"How did you get in there?" Greta puzzled, stroked the big yellow cat. "I bet you are ever so hungry."

The way that Caliph lapped eagerly at the saucer of milk in the kitchen confirmed Greta's guess. She sat on the floor watching him eat. She felt very proud and self-sufficient suddenly. It would have been awful if she had awakened Mother.

When Caliph was quite through with the milk,

Greta lifted him out of her bedroom window and set him on the fire escape. He sat a moment washing himself daintily before he started down the stairs. He paused at every landing and walked delicately on the stairs between.

As Greta was much to wide-awake to go back to bed yet, she watched Caliph descend until he reached the level of Miss Gray's apartment. He had only become settled well, with his paws nestled cozily under his round chest, when Miss Gray noticed him. The window opened with a bang and Miss Gray, her head greatly oversized from curlers covered by a purple scarf, drew Caliph inside with a welcome cry.

"This is like a story," Greta thought with satisfaction, yawning a little when Miss Gray's light finally went out. "And it all ended so happily."

The question itself came slowly, stirring in Greta's head until she finally sat up in bed to think it through. "A proper story," she concluded finally, whispering to the empty room and to the wisp of white curtain moving uncertainly against the open window. "But a really proper story shouldn't leave a wiggle of a question still hanging in the air." Greta asked herself the question aloud, "How did

Caliph get into the wall behind the closet?"

Sitting in the silent room, Greta thought about the door. She knew without a doubt that she could not sleep until she had had one good peek.

Strangely enough she felt quite brave, getting the flashlight from the kitchen and working to jiggle the door open. She had slammed it very hard when Caliph had jumped out at her.

It was quite a small opening, barely large enough to squeeze through.

"I don't have any business here," Greta told herself firmly as the door came loose. "I'll just take a quick peek."

Around the door's entrance there was only dust, so much dust that Greta's nose wriggled miserably toward a sneeze. The rafters angled off sharply from the height of the closet and were wreathed with great canopies of forgotten spider webs glowing a chalky white in the flashlight's beam.

Greta moved the circle of light slowly. Then it stopped suddenly. For one terrible moment Greta did not think she could control the scream that wanted to escape from her throat. Instead she closed her eyes quickly and slammed the door shut, even harder than before.

After she had escaped from the closet she considered her room quickly for a moment with her heart pounding very hard.

She wished that she could push her heavy chest of drawers up against the closet door so as to keep it shut tight. But Mother would be sure to ask questions about that. Then Greta saw the closet key. Although she had never used it, it had hung by the closet door as long as she could remember. Greta sighed with relief as she turned it in the lock. Now Mother would never have to know how frightened she had been.

A milk truck rattled along far up the street and the early workers were honking their way through the dim dawn light far below, before Greta finally fell asleep.

Mother looked at her critically during breakfast. "You really don't look as if you feel well, honey," she told Greta. "Would you like to stay home and rest quietly today?"

"Oh, no, thank you," Greta told her quickly. That was just the very last thing in the whole wide world that she wanted to do—stay alone in the little apartment all day with that closet door. "May I play with Peter after school?" she asked.

Mother smiled warmly. "Of course you may. Greta, I'm sorry about yesterday, but girls must learn to be neat, you know. Maybe you just look peaked from missing that day of sunshine. You and Peter may play right up to dinner time if you wish."

When Greta kissed her mother good-bye she felt a little mixed up. She must tell someone about the thing behind the closet door, but somehow Mother did not seem to be the right one. Maybe Peter. Peter was wise in a boy's way, and, if there happened to be some nice dull answer to her question, Peter would find it right away. He was great at making even the most exciting things seem dull if he had not thought of them first.

When Greta rapped at Peter's door it opened at once. She almost tumbled back, Peter came out so quickly.

"Whatever do you know!" Greta exclaimed with a grin. "Peter on time."

The face Peter made at her made all the freckles on his nose seem to run together.

"Mind your manners or walk to school alone," he said, grinning back to show that what she had said did not really matter.

Greta remembered what she had said to him about a secret the day before. Peter would never admit it, but she was sure that it was curiosity that had made him get ready on time for a change. And to think that she had had no secret when she said it, and now the secret was too big to want to tell!

Mrs. Trainor was sweeping the downstairs hall when they reached the final flight of stairs. They waited on the bottom step until her broom had swished their way clear. She smiled up at them sweetly, but Greta noticed that she looked very tired.

"How are you today?" Peter asked politely. Peter's manners were always in the best of condition, Greta thought, giggling to herself, because he used them so seldom. But Mrs. Trainor somehow brought out the very best in him.

"Very well, thank you, Peter, and you?" she asked gently. Greta sighed. She loved the way Mrs. Trainor's words came out slow and soft from a deep place of breathing that made them sound different from other people's words.

"Fine, thank you," Peter answered. "Did Miss Gray find her cat?"

Mrs. Trainor's smile widened and she was about to answer when Greta spoke without thinking. "Yes, she did, and she was sure glad to see him, too."

When they both looked at her questioningly,

Greta felt suddenly embarrassed. She had no reason to be downstairs early enough to see Miss Gray leave for her job. Of course they must be wondering how she knew.

"Something woke me in the night and I was looking out of the window when Miss Gray found him on the fire escape," Greta explained quite honestly. It was truthful, she told herself defensively, flushing in spite of herself. Not all the truth maybe, but the truth.

A little line of worry fretted Mrs. Trainor's face under the high pompadour of white curls that piled about her forehead. She cocked her head slightly, looking at Greta sympathetically. "I've heard strange noises a couple of nights myself," she said. "They seem to come from higher up, so they must be louder where you are."

"I never hear a thing but Greta's snoring, myself," Peter complained clownishly.

Mrs. Trainor's laugh was so quick and musical that it filled the whole hall, making it seem brighter. "Oh, Peter, you are such a tease." she said merrily. "Go on to school and learn better manners."

She poked him with her broom and they left laughing.

"I sure wish we could give her a hand," Peter said solemnly as they crossed the street. "I like her so much."

"I do too," Greta agreed. "But a hand with what? Finding whatever it is that she's looking for?"

This was a strange thing about Mrs. Trainor. Other older ladies who lived in the house did quiet things. They sat and crocheted or read their newspapers. But Mrs. Trainor looked. No one knew what she was looking for, but you could almost hear her. There would be a little swish or a bang as if drawers were being opened and closed unhappily. Sometimes when Greta stopped in to call on her, Mrs. Trainor would come from another room. In an open closet door, Greta would see a chair. She felt as if she had interrupted Mrs. Trainor in the act of searching her own closet shelves.

"I don't know what she's looking for," Peter said shortly, "but it's money that she needs. Dad said that if she doesn't fix this place up, it's going to be condemned. There are old timbers and other things that don't meet the city's Fire Department regulations. It would take a pile of money." Peter hesitated a moment. "I wish I could earn some to give to her."

"Maybe the rent money will take care of it," Greta said hopefully, trying to believe that this new information was just a rumor. "Mother says rents are very high."

"So are taxes, and Mrs. Trainor shares the income with her sisters who live off in Florida somewhere," Peter said defensively.

The idea of Mrs. Trainor's losing the house was such an unhappy thought that Greta walked along silently for a moment. It just could not be. The house was so beautiful and so exciting to live in. Where else could you walk through rooms where such famous people had lived and had fun together? There were the neighbors, too. Greta loved them all, especially Mr. Wong at the laundry with his smooth, cream-colored face that broke into a wide, friendly smile below his slanted black eyes.

"Oh, Peter," Greta said miserably. "I don't want to move, ever."

"We'll all have to," Peter grumbled, "unless something is done about that old house." Greta glanced up at him just in time to see the sly look he was giving her as he added, "I thought maybe your secret was something about moving."

Greta wished instantly that he had not mentioned it. Now they were on the school grounds and there would not be time to tell him about the little door. Just remembering what she had seen made tingles of fear run cold inside her jumper blouse.

"I can play after school," she told him quickly, as some of her friends left a group in the schoolyard and started toward them. "I'll tell you then."

One nice thing about arithmetic and spelling and remembering how to write the names of South American countries is that they push other things right out of your head, Greta thought. Not until the rush of the last bell did Greta remember to shiver about the closet door again.

For a wonder, Peter seemed to have forgotten about it, too.

"Do you want to play a game, going home?" Peter asked as they left together.

"If you do," Greta agreed amiably. After all, she might just as well wait until they got home and tell him there. Then she would not have to think about it for that much longer.

"I've thought of a neat new way to play Alphabet," Peter said eagerly. "Instead of just saying something that begins with the right letter, you have to go and touch it and then go on from there."

"What if it's a fire engine?" Greta giggled. "We'd have to run like fury."

"Oh, don't be silly," Peter said. "We could make it a rule that we can't leave the block we're in to find it. Maybe we could go around the block, but not leave it."

"Who gets to start?" Greta hinted.

"Girls first," Peter grinned," but just for today."

Greta looked only a moment before walking straight to the applecart where a sober little man stood with his hands folded together under his apron.

"A is for applecart," she said, smiling at the man as she touched his wagon. He smiled back when he realized they were playing a game.

"I'm the base, huh?" he asked cheerfully. "But it's bananas, too."

"B for bananas," Peter exclaimed with a yelp. "That was easy."

Greta touched a car for C at the curb. Then there was D for the door of the drug store, and E for an empty candy wrapper someone had dropped on the sidewalk. F was hard until Peter reminded Greta of the fireplug just around the corner.

They did not generally go around the back way

to get home, but the game made it necessary today.

They were still a few feet from the fireplug when Peter said, "Look there's an artist."

When Greta looked, she gave an exclamation of surprise. "Why, that's Mrs. Owens," she whispered to Peter. "She lives in our house, in the apartment with the polka-dotted curtains."

Peter started walking toward the woman quickly, and there was nothing for Greta to do but follow him and try to keep up.

Mrs. Owens was using a sketch pad, holding its

stiff back against her left arm. She kept looking up, craning her head at an odd angle, then adding quick lines to the picture.

"What are you drawing?" Peter asked cordially. Apparently Mrs. Owens had not noticed their approach because she flushed angrily and frowned, covering the picture with her arm swiftly.

"None of your business." She glared at Peter crossly. After giving Greta a strange, annoyed look, Mrs. Owens closed the sketch book under her arm and walked off swiftly.

Peter stared after the woman in surprise. "Not very friendly, your Mrs. Owens," he commented.

Greta did not answer. She was craning her head just as Mrs. Owens had done. "I was right, then," she muttered. The woman's drawing had looked just like the back of the Trainor house to her. Standing here, with her head cocked just right, Greta found that she had a perfect view of the topmost story of the Trainor house. She could even see the edge of her own window.

A little shiver of fear moved inside Greta. Why would Mrs. Owens be drawing her window? And why was she so angry when they found her doing it?

🏰🏰 3 🏰🏰

"And I don't even think she draws very well," Peter added, looking after Mrs. Owens who was disappearing down the street.

"She borrowed an egg from me yesterday," Greta said slowly, her mind on the curious woman's visit.

Peter wrinkled his face at her before laughing out loud. "Borrowing eggs always keeps a person from being a good artist," he said soberly.

Greta grinned sheepishly at him. "Let's cut through the alley going home," she suggested. "I want to tell you my secret, and you can help me solve a mystery."

Peter's round face brightened with excitement

at the word "mystery" and he looked at her eagerly. "What kind of mystery? he asked quickly.

Greta told him about the door behind the closet wallpaper and how Caliph had escaped from the place when it was opened. She had reached the point of telling him how she had gone back to take another peek when she suddenly stopped.

"Come on, Greta, what did you see?" he asked impatiently.

Greta bit her lip hesitantly. "Promise me you won't laugh," she said slowly. "It seems so silly to say it out loud now. But it wasn't silly last night," she added defensively.

"I won't laugh," Peter promised eagerly. "Just tell me what you saw."

"I'm not sure, of course; it was so dark and the place is small and there was only the flashlight."

"Greta," Peter said warningly, his eyes round above his freckles.

"It was like a man," Greta said slowly. "with a hat above where his head would be, and instead of a face . . ." she hesitated, looking appealingly at him.

"Instead of a face was a what?" Peter pressed, almost jumping up and down with suspense.

"A star," Greta said firmly, and glared at him.

"A star," Peter squeaked unbelievingly. "A star in a hole in your closet under a man's hat?"

Greta nodded numbly. "You promised not to laugh," she added.

"I'm not laughing," Peter said slowly. "I'm just surprised." They were at the side of the Trainor house now and Greta watched Peter. His round face was serious as he looked up the fire escape to the topmost story.

Then he slumped down on the bottom step and put his chin in his hands. Greta sat down beside him. She felt better now that she had told him right out about the figure in the closet, but really it would be better if Peter had laughed instead of looking so serious.

"Peter," she said slowly.

"I'm thinking," he replied firmly. Greta waited.

"The noises stopped as soon as you let Caliph out?" he asked after a bit.

"That's right," Greta answered meekly.

"How loud were the noises? Loud enough for Mrs. Trainor to hear from the first floor?"

Greta stared at him. "Of course not, silly. They would have wakened Mother and everyone else if they were."

"I didn't laugh at you, so you better not call me

silly," Peter flared defensively. "I'm working on a theory."

"Tell me," Greta coaxed.

"Not just yet. Come on."

Peter was generally the slow one, but this time Greta found herself panting as she followed his rapid two-at-a-time progress up the stairs. He stopped red-faced in front of Greta's door at the topmost story.

"Are you going to investigate my closet?" Greta asked, unlocking the door.

"Not just yet. I want to look around outside and I hate climbing that old fire escape."

Greta watched from her room as Peter climbed out her window onto the fire escape and poked and pried and peered about. When a sudden knock came on her door, she pulled her head in quickly and went to answer it.

Mrs. Owens stood in the hall with an egg in her hand. She wore a very friendly look all over her face except for her eyes which peered curiously about the living room as before. "Here's your egg, dearie," she said kindly. "It certainly saved my pudding." Greta did not even have time to say "Thank you" before the woman's voice hurried on.

"I'm sorry I was so rude to you kids a while ago.

You scared me, coming up suddenly like that. And it's just that I don't draw well enough to let anyone see my work."

"I'm sorry we startled you," Greta answered. "But I just love to watch people draw."

"Most people do, I guess," Mrs. Owens said. "As I said before, I'm not much at drawing but I sure like to do it. And I especially like to draw old houses."

She hesitated, and Greta felt that she was expected to say something. But she kept thinking of Peter out on the fire escape and wondering what he was finding. Once having apologized, Mrs. Owens seemed relaxed and eager to visit.

"Well," the woman said, after Greta stood awkwardly silent a minute. "Thanks for the egg, and remember, if you ever need anything, just come and ask."

"I will, thank you," Greta said, closing the door gratefully and hurrying back to check on Peter.

She was startled to find him gone.

When she could see no sign of him anywhere, even down below, she called out quickly, "Peter, Peter, where are you?"

"Look up here." His voice came strangely from above her head.

"Get off that roof!" Greta yelled almost angrily. It frightened her to see him stretched on the roof above her with his freckled face red from hanging it over the edge.

"I will in a minute," he answered cheerfully. "But look over there."

He pointed to a place way back among the eaves several feet away from the fire escape. In among the fancy curls of old wood whose paint was scaling in the overhang of the eaves, Greta saw what Peter was pointing at. It was a little opening set in the wall with slanted slats across it.

"It's just a ventilator," she told him.

"Just a ventilator," Peter repeated wisely, springing down beside her on the fire escape landing. "And you really have to look to find it, too." Greta thought he was uncommonly puffed up with this achievement.

"I knew there had to be an outside opening for Caliph to crawl through and for you to see a star," he said.

"But that's been there forever," Greta said. "Why didn't he find his way in before?"

"For the same reason you couldn't have seen the star before," Peter said smugly.

"For that matter, I couldn't see a star through

that thing anyway," Greta said, feeling a little annoyed at his boasting tone. "Those little slats are slanted down to keep the rain out."

"They used to be," Peter said triumphantly. "But they've been sawed through and very recently, from the looks of them. Someone has pulled them out at the far end, and there's a hole plenty big enough for Caliph."

Greta followed Peter back in through her apartment. His face was tight with his thinking look as she asked, "But why would anyone want to saw them through, way up there like that?"

Peter shrugged very grandly, then added with a grin, whispering, "To let that closet man in maybe."

"Peter," Greta wailed.

"Oh, Greta," Peter said teasingly. "Nobody but a cat could get in through that ventilator. You saw how little it is. But there's still something mighty strange about this. Maybe it was the sawing sound that Mrs. Trainor heard instead of Caliph. Sawing would sound clearer from the outside than from within, and it wouldn't sound like a cat scratching a wall."

"Do you want to look in there now?" Greta

asked tremulously, not much wanting to have the little door opened again for anything.

"Sure thing," Peter replied. "Then we ought to tell Mrs. Trainor about the ventilator. If there are such things going on, she should know."

Peter returned to Greta's closet door, and she admired the quick, brave way he started to turn her door handle. Then he frowned at her. "Hey, it's locked," he said, surprised.

"I'm sorry, I forgot," Greta said, giggling. A little flustered, she started looking for the key. "I know I put it somewhere safe," she said, looking through her jewelry box. "Maybe the kitchen. "She ran out quickly to look. Peter seemed very annoyed at her.

"Gosh, Peter," Greta said as he followed her into the kitchen. "I remember plain as anything that I left it here on the window sill and now it's gone."

"Why would you put it there?"

"I was holding it and wondering what to do when Mother called me to breakfast." Greta remembered it very clearly now. "I put it up there when I washed my hands."

"Well, if that isn't the dumbest thing!" Peter

exploded angrily. Then he grinned. "All I have to say is that you'd better locate it this evening. We can't do a thing about the mystery if we can't get into your closet."

"Mother probably moved it and she'll know where it is," Greta said, secretly glad she did not have to go into the closet today. There really would not be much time anyway. It was almost dusk and her mother and Peter's parents would be home from work soon.

"Well." Peter shrugged. "Let's go tell Mrs. Trainor about the ventilator. We can do that much."

Usually Mrs. Trainor answered quickly when anyone rapped at her door. She would pull it open almost silently and say, "Yes?" in her wonderful, soft voice. But although Greta and Peter rapped twice, quite loudly the second time, there was no answer from behind the hall door.

"Maybe she's busy and doesn't hear," Greta suggested. She leaned her finger heavily against the button near Mrs. Trainor's mailbox. They heard the squeal of the buzzer deep in the back of the apartment, but no vibration of feet came to answer it.

Peter shrugged. "There's no law that says she can't go out sometimes."

"She usually stays in afternoons," Greta said.

"We can check around the neighborhood; maybe she's out shopping," Peter suggested.

"Haven't seen Mrs. Trainor for a long time," Mr. Grant in the bakery told them. "Miss her, too, such a nice lady. She comes in once in a while for bread. She should be almost out of it now," he added hopefully. He flattened his broad red hands on his white apron. "You kids want a doughnut hole?" he asked, grinning.

The bakery smells made Peter and Greta both very hungry. They accepted the sugary rounds eagerly.

"Try Mr. Wong," Mr. Grant suggested, slipping the tray back into the showcase. "I noticed the curtains were down in the Trainor place a few minutes ago when I was fixing my awning. Maybe Mrs. Trainor took them over for him to wash."

Peter and Greta ate slowly to make their treat last. "No doughnut hands on clean clothes," Mr. Wong called warningly as they entered his shop. "Mrs. Trainor? Not for long time." He shook his head as emphatically as Mr. Grant had. Everyone knew Mrs. Trainor and remembered her calls.

Something kept bothering Greta. She couldn't remember whether it was something she had seen or heard or what. When they had made the rounds of the entire neighborhood, they had to conclude that Mrs. Trainor had gone farther than a simple shopping trip.

Returning home, they patted Caliph who was on the outside steps, before entering the darkening hallway. At the first breath of inside air, Greta knew what had been bothering her.

"Gas," she said to Peter quickly. "I smell gas. I smelled it before when we were here."

Peter sniffed noisily. "Where do you think it's coming from?" he asked after a minute. There were three small apartments on the ground floor. When Peter held his nose close to the door of the Trainor apartment, there was no reason to look further. He drew back gasping and coughing.

"Run around outside, Greta," he said. "Try to get a window up while I see if I can force this door."

Greta stumbled over Caliph, still curled on the steps. She tugged at the little front windows but they were locked tight. It was so frustrating to look through the glass and see the locks slipped tidily into their little grooves.

Then she noticed the curtainless window that Mr. Grant had mentioned. Hooding her face with her hands, she peered inside. "Peter," she yelled desperately. "Peter, come quickly."

Inside Greta could see Mrs. Trainor lying on the floor with her eyes shut. All about her in great disorder was a tangle of white curtains. An upsidedown teakettle lay in a pool of water on the floor with a spoon beside it.

"Your shoe," Peter yelled, the moment he joined her at the window. "And stand back."

When he struck the window with Greta's loafer, a shower of glass went everywhere. The sound attracted a couple of men.

"Hey what are you kids up to?" one of the men called angrily. "Call a cop!" he ordered his companion, as he started towards them.

"A cop," Greta thought with relief. "That would be Officer Mullens and he'll know just what to do."

But Peter was not waiting for help. He cleared the broken glass from the window and clambered through. Greta followed him just as the strange man reached them. Peter knelt on the floor and

began to call to Mrs. Trainor very urgently, hoping to arouse her.

The man coughed a little and blinked steadily when he got inside. He quickly checked the flow of gas by turning off the front jet on the little stove. Then he moved about swiftly, opening windows to clear the gas from the air in the apartment.

With everything happening so fast, Greta was terribly confused. And she was right about Officer Mullens. When he arrived, he got Mrs. Trainor propped up on the living room love seat. By the time the siren of the emergency ambulance was wailing out front, Mrs. Trainor was shaking her head with its little pompadour of white curls and trying to get her eyes open.

She was not really herself yet, you could tell that. She kept repeating peculiar things as if she were unsure of where she was. No one seemed to be listening to her but Greta. The two men who had seen Peter break the windows were telling Officer Mullens all about that. "These kids saved that old lady's life," one of them said, looking admiringly at Peter and Greta. "They broke that window and got the air into this place just in the nick of time."

"And you say the gas was still on when you followed them in?" Officer Mullen asked, looking up from Mrs. Trainor's side where he was briskly rubbing her badly swollen ankle.

"It looked as if she had tried to get something out of that cabinet over the stove," one man explained. "Lost her balance. You know how women will climb on chairs. She must have knocked the gas jet open falling against it."

Probably because the emergency ambulance was parked in front of the Trainor house, a sizable crowd of people gathered outside. Officer Mullens left Mrs. Trainor's a couple of times to tell the peo-

ple to move on. When he was finally convinced that she would recover without a trip to the hospital, he sent the ambulance away.

After five o'clock the people of the Trainor house began arriving from work. As they passed the open door they could see past Officer Mullens in his trim uniform to where Mrs. Trainor was propped on the love seat. All of them stopped to inquire and stayed to offer help and sympathy.

Miss Gray arrived and fluttered about, talking constantly and managing to be wherever Officer Mullens wanted to turn. She kept suggesting things

that Mrs. Trainor needed—a cup of strong tea, or a bowl of hot soup. Greta almost giggled when Officer Mullens, with fine control of his voice suggested earnestly that she go right upstairs and fix it herself. She trotted off obediently, mumbling happily to Caliph who was draped tiredly over her arm.

But even with Miss Gray gone, the usually quiet rooms seemed confused. Greta's mother had arrived from work and had gone straight into the kitchen to put it to rights again. She mopped up the spilled water and, with Peter's help, got the curtains back on their damaged rods.

Mrs. Trainor seemed wide awake now and her blue eyes looked about unhappily.

"How dreadful to cause so much commotion," she apologized to the room at large. "I just felt myself slipping and grabbed at those curtains."

"Just so you are all right now," Officer Mullens said gravely. His pen wobbled busily as he filled out his report form. When it was completed, the two men left. Soon the rooms were practically empty except for a few tenants standing about uneasily waiting for a chance to say their good-byes to Mrs. Trainor.

"There's your artist friend," Peter said, nudging Greta. Peter was right. Mrs. Owens was among the people still in the room. It annoyed Greta that Mrs. Owens seemed to be paying no attention to Mrs. Trainor or to the police officer. Instead, her bright eyes were moving curiously over the books on the shelf and roving quickly about the apartment.

"She's nosy," Greta whispered to Peter. "She acts as if she doesn't even care that Mrs. Trainor could have been hurt badly."

"I'd be mighty proud of that pair if they were mine," Officer Mullens told Greta's mother as she came from the kitchen. "How come you kids ever noticed anything was wrong?"

"We had to see Mrs. Trainor and she didn't answer her bell," Peter explained.

"When we got back from asking for her around the neighborhood, we smelled gas," Greta went on.

"Did you want me for something special?" Mrs. Trainor asked gently from where she sat with her injured ankle resting on a rose-colored cushion. She still looked very pale and ill, Greta thought.

"Nothing that's important now," Peter answered quickly, exchanging a glance with Greta.

"And as for you, Little Lady," Officer Mullens

said to Mrs. Trainor grimly, "you stay off chairs when you are here alone."

"I'm sorry," Mrs. Trainor answered meekly. "I just climbed up there to look for something."

Greta left with her mother when Miss Gray bustled in carrying a tray covered with a white cloth. Greta was very thoughtful all the way upstairs. Now she and Peter had a new riddle to solve along with last night's old one.

Usually Greta would have listened eagerly to the loving, proud words that her mother was saying as they mounted the stairs together. But this time Greta only nodded absently as her mother's voice went on tenderly. Greta's mind was on another voice. She shook her head wonderingly as she repeated to herself the words that Mrs. Trainor had said over and over.

"So bright, so beautiful, a star for a star." What could they mean, these confused words spoken in Mrs. Trainor's soft voice?

4

"*Did your mother know any-*thing about the key?" Peter asked, catching up with Greta outside of school the next afternoon.

"Oh, Peter, you'll be mad! I forgot to ask her. I was so upset about Mrs. Trainor, and then I over-slept and put the same clothes back on this morning."

"It's very easy to derail a one-track mind," Peter said disgustedly.

"You needn't be that way," Greta protested. "I was scared that night."

"That's easy to understand," Peter conceded. "But you will ask her tonight for sure? Promise."

"Promise," Greta agreed solemnly.

"Let's go and see how Mrs. Trainor is feeling," Peter suggested.

"That's a good idea," Greta agreed. "Are you going to tell her about the ventilator?"

Peter frowned, his round face wrinkled with indecision. "Maybe yes and maybe no," he answered slowly. "Let's wait and see how she feels. Those bars won't let anything bigger than a cat through anyway; the opening is just too small."

"Then the only way for a person to get into that place," Greta said slowly, "would be through the door in the back of my closet."

"That's right," Peter said cheerfully. From the way he was eyeing her, Greta knew that her fear had shown in her voice. "Go look at that ventilator yourself if you aren't afraid to climb the roof."

"I'll take your word for it," Greta laughed.

They had barely finished knocking when Mrs. Trainor's soft voice spoke from the doorway.

"Peter and Greta," she exclaimed with delight, as if they were her favorite surprise to find in her front hall. "This has been a wonderful day. So many callers, and now you have come!"

"We wanted to see how you were feeling," Greta

told her. Peter was too overcome with pleasure at
Mrs. Trainor's happy, approving glance to say
anything.

"Do come in and visit with me," she said graciously. "As far as my feelings, I am halfway up and
halfway down. I feel much better than I did last
night and not nearly so good as I shall tomorrow.
My ankle still hurts when I walk or stand on it."
She chuckled when she said this, as if nothing in
the world were less important.

Mrs. Trainor motioned Peter and Greta to vel-
vet-covered chairs whose arched backs were carved
with softly rounded roses. Then, cocking her head
with its pile of soft, white curls, she said quizzi-
cally, "Every quiet moment of this day I have
thought of you two. I have been trying to think
of how to thank you for saving me from what could
have been quite terrible, you know."

Although the words were said lightly, almost
gaily, Greta saw a much different feeling in Mrs.
Trainor's blue eyes.

"All we want to know is that you're okay," Peter
stammered, blushing.

"Peter, Peter," Mrs. Trainor sighed, shaking her
head and smiling. "How charming to have friends

like you who say such tender things with such awk-
ward words as 'Okay'!" As she said it, she rounded
her mouth into an "O" and shook her shoulders
for all the world like a ruffian. Peter and Greta both
laughed with her.

"I almost forgot." She jumped to her feet and
with quick grace, in spite of her slight limp, went
flying into the kitchen. Her words flowed back to
them through the open door. "For once I have
goodies to offer my wonderful friends."

She returned carrying a gold-trimmed china
serving dish with an assortment of cookies arranged
on it. "Choose what you wish." She held the tray
invitingly toward Greta. "Those lovely chocolate
ones are from Mr. Grant at the bakery. He came in
a while ago to bring them to me with his best
wishes."

"And these?" Greta asked curiously, picking up
a pastry that was like a tiny, crisp, baked envelope
with a little roll of parchment sticking out of the
end.

"That's a Chinese fortune cooky." Mrs. Trainor
smiled. "Mr. Wong also called today and brought
me those. He knows how dearly I love them."

"Why do they call them fortune cookies?" Peter

asked, coming over to stare at the little pastry in Greta's hand.

Quickly Mrs. Trainor broke the little cooky and unrolled the tiny scroll of paper inside it. Her blue eyes fixed on it curiously a moment before she handed it to Greta. "This must be your fortune, my dear. It can't be mine." She sighed a little wistfully as she said it.

"You will find happiness where you least expect it," Greta read aloud. "Oh, that's nice."

"That could be true for anybody," Peter said comfortingly.

Mrs. Trainor sighed, placing her slender hands on the sides of her head as if it were a goblet filled with something precious. "All this day my head has been overflowing with memories," she said gently. "Some noise from the street this morning sounded for a minute like the hoofs of a horse. It was as if all the years had been swept away and the hansom cabs were passing along the street under the gaslight, bringing the whole cast of the play to my house to dine."

Greta held the half-eaten cooky forgotten in her hand. She felt a tug of sudden excitement. This was the play world she loved so dearly, the world of make-believe that she walked into at the door of the Trainor house whenever she walked in alone. From Peter's expression it looked as if he too were reaching back in time to the New York of dim gas lights and the rackety rhythm of horses' hoofs.

"Was it very wonderful?" Greta asked wistfully.

"Very wonderful," Mrs. Trainor echoed with satisfaction. "And it still seems so real to me. Why, just today a man came to pay the rent, the new man upstairs. Standing there in the hall, he seemed for a moment like an unsmiling ghost. He reminded me that strongly of a friend of those old days."

Then it was as if she and Peter had gone from the room, Greta realized, and as if all the years had fled with them. Mrs. Trainor sat, gracefully relaxed, with slim hands resting folded in her lap, while her eyes brightened with the magic of her memories.

"And all so romantic," she said softly. She cocked her head at them curiously. "I wonder if you can imagine how it was. There were three worlds." She put the tips of her fingers together as she talked, as if each of these remembered worlds were right there, spinning inside the circle of her hands.

"In the world behind the footlights, we lived the play. We were like little figures inside a glass paperweight. The story swirled around us and made us alive in it for that time." She smiled suddenly. "And beyond the lights was the world of the audience. It was all faces—laughing faces, crying faces, and sometimes silent faces. This was what we liked best. When the faces were so still, we knew that the audience was caught in the spell of the story, and a little of the stage world would go home with them to stay."

"And then," she leaned forward breathlessly, "we came back to the world that was our very own. All of the ladies were in fancy dresses and wore plumed hats. In our jeweled splendor we would pile into the carriages and come here to dine.

"The food would taste wonderful, and the talk would be so sparkling that the flames of the candles would sway with the breath of our laughter, as if they were bowing and taking encores. But boys are not romantic," she said suddenly, with a glance of apology at Peter. "Still there were exciting things that you would have liked, too. Once there was a prince from a small Balkan country. His nation is now only a flag in a history book. The uniform he wore made even our stage costumes look drab, and the jewels in his scabbard shone like stars when he rose to applaud us."

Greta watched Mrs. Trainor curiously. Once she had asked Mother how old Mrs. Trainor was. Mother had puzzled a moment before making a guess.

"Probably in her early seventies," she had said finally. "I remember that she was already a star on the stage when she was eighteen. She was married to Mr. Trainor during World War I, and that was before I was born."

It was hard for Greta to believe that Mrs. Trainor could be that old. Her eyes were so bright when she talked, and her smile was as soft as a happy girl's face.

"Did you get to meet this prince?" Peter asked, impressed.

Mrs. Trainor chuckled again. "He asked permission to join us at dinner." She added with amusement, "A plump minister in his party kept going to sleep. He would waken suddenly, blinking like an owl in the sunlight. He would say, 'yes, sir, yes, sir,' as if he had been spoken to. Even before we had finished laughing at him he would be asleep again, his head rolling upon his neck like a bobbing apple."

"What fun it must have been," Peter agreed, his eyes wrinkling with laughter.

"After the prince sailed away home," Mrs. Trainor went on, "there came a wooden chest by messenger. He had said 'Thank you' in the very loveliest way, with jewels from his kingdom." Greta saw a little worried frown crease her face briefly.

"Too bad that I can't show you all these things," she said fretfully. "For a long time I kept every gown that I played in." She turned to Greta. "Why, there was a fortune just in those lovely clothes. I had my favorites, of course. One that I especially liked was ruined at a performance one night. It was a queen's dress. The fabric was velvet and had real jewels set in its great skirt to catch the light. One night when the whole cast was on stage a heavy curtain fell. Everyone ran screaming as the huge curtain bar came rumbling down. It would have crushed anyone caught under it. I escaped," she smiled, "but my skirt was ripped off and I fled from the stage in my petticoats."

"I bet the audience went wild," Peter remarked.

"That's a good way to describe it," she agreed.

"But we cleared the stage and the show went on. It was our way, you know.

"Maybe falling curtains are my bad luck sign," she added brightly. "It was the curtain I caught at that let me down yesterday."

Peter laughed at her pun. "Have you got that all fixed now?"

"Not really," Mrs. Trainor said. "The rod is still bent and the slightest jar will make it come loose. I thought I would wait until my ankle healed to get another from the storage room in the basement."

"I'll get one for you," Peter offered, rising immediately.

"That would be nice," Mrs. Trainor said. "But look, it's getting dark outside and your mothers will expect you. If you don't mind, though, maybe tomorrow?"

"Just depend on me," Peter said importantly.

Greta wanted terribly to let Mrs. Trainor know how wonderful the afternoon had been, but the words would not come out right. Greta felt that she had been too far away to return so quickly to the reality of speaking everyday words.

As she left, Greta laid her hand for a moment

on Mrs. Trainor's arm helplessly. "Thank you so much for sharing your memories," she said slowly. "I loved it so."

Mrs. Trainor studied her face a moment, then leaned and pressed her cheek against Greta's. "Thank you for caring," she said softly, just before she disappeared inside her door.

"It's ever so much later than I thought," Peter said as they started up the stairs. "This must really have been some place in those days, huh, Greta?"

"It still is," Greta answered defensively. "I would love to see those clothes she wore."

"And that jewelled scabbard of the prince's," Peter added, patting his hip loudly. "Maybe I can tell her about the ventilator bars tomorrow," Peter suggested as they parted at his door. "I'll have to be there about the curtain rods anyway."

Greta was surprised to find the apartment still empty when she let herself in. It was past the time when Mother usually got home. Greta set the table carefully and put on the water for her mother's tea. The kettle was just beginning to sing when she heard her mother's cheery voice from the living room.

"Hope you didn't worry," her mother called

quickly, hanging up her coat and coming to join Greta in the kitchen.

"I haven't been here long myself," Greta admitted. "Peter and I stopped to visit Mrs. Trainor and stayed all afternoon."

"Heavens!" her mother looked at her in dismay. "I hope you children aren't making pests of yourselves."

"I don't think so," Greta replied slowly. "She was telling us about the long ago when she was an actress and this whole mansion was her home."

"You love this place, don't you, Greta?" Mother asked, stopping her swift hands to stare at Greta curiously.

"I really do," Greta replied solemnly. "I think it's wonderful." Except for that part behind the door in the closet, she added to herself guiltily.

Her mother sighed. "Wait until we can move out to a certain little village back in Vermont. You would *really* find that life wonderful, Greta. And anyway, dear, unless this building gets a lot of work done on it, I'm afraid it's doomed."

"I don't really understand that," Greta admitted. "You mean it isn't safe for us to live here?"

"Oh, it isn't all that bad yet," her mother replied.

"But it's my understanding that if Mrs. Trainor doesn't have a lot of major work done, the building inspectors will not let her rent the apartments for another year."

In spite of herself, Greta felt hot tears forming behind her eyes. "But it's our home," she wailed. "And it's so full of memories that I love every inch of it."

"I'm glad you do, Greta," Mother said gently. "We are going to stay here for a while anyway, unless we *have* to move. I do so hate the job of moving. That's what I told that new lady downstairs."

Greta had a quick question for her mother, but the telephone rang. By the time Mother came back, Greta had started the dishes and had quite forgotten what it was that she was going to ask.

She was lucky enough to remember her promise to Peter.

"Mother, did you see the key to my closet door?" she asked when her mother came back from the telephone. "I'm sure I left it on the windowsill, but it's not here."

"Oh, was that your key?" Mother asked. "I noticed it there and put it in my dresser drawer. Are you locking your closet these days?" She said it so jokingly that Greta suddenly felt very bad about keeping the secret from her.

"It was a silly thing to do," Greta answered. "But it was even sillier to find the key gone and not be able to unlock it."

Mother laughed, getting the key out for her. "That explains why my little peacock wore the same dress to school twice."

It was after she had gone to bed and was lying listening to the far noises of the city street settling for the night that Greta remembered the other question she had meant to ask her mother.

The bed was so snugly warm that she first thought of waiting and asking her mother at breakfast. Finally her curiosity won.

Mother was half asleep when Greta padded in to sit by her on the bed.

"Something wrong, dear?" Mother asked gently, reaching a sleep-lazed hand up to Greta's hair.

"Not really," Greta answered." I just wanted to know what you were about to tell me this evening when the telephone rang. Something about the new woman downstairs and moving."

Greta's mother laughed softly into the dark.

"That was nothing to get up for, really. It was just such a silly thing for anyone to suggest. The new woman walked upstairs with me when I came home. She asked if I would like to trade apartments with her."

"Trade apartments? What did she mean?" Greta asked.

"Oh, they would take ours and we would take theirs, that's all," her mother explained. "But what made it so silly was that she offered to pay the difference in rent if I'd swap apartments."

"Who was she?" Greta asked, although she was frighteningly sure that she already knew.

"I didn't even ask her name," Mother said softly. "She's blond with a round face, rather like a doll. But the whole idea was so silly that I didn't take it seriously at all."

She pulled Greta down and kissed her gently. "Now, hop to bed, Greta-pet. Tomorrow will be an early school day for you. Come to think of it, though, it's really very strange," she yawned sleepily. "What possible reason would anyone have to want to pay extra rent for the topmost story?"

Greta snuggled deep in the covers of her bed. Even knowing the closet door was locked did not help very much. She kept remembering her talk with Peter about that place behind her closet. It was as if the words were being repeated in the quiet of her room. "The only way to get in is through the back of that closet."

"Tomorrow," Greta promised herself miserably. "Tomorrow Peter and I will go in there and investigate, no matter what."

ᛗ ᛗ 5 ᛗ ᛗ

Because it was raining, Peter and
Greta ran all the way home. The sky looked like
smudged pencil marks and the rain was falling
straight down as if the raindrops knew that if they
blew this way or that, they would never find the
darkening sidewalks between the tall buildings.
The children stood inside the hall a minute, trem-
bling from dampness and shaking themselves like
uncomfortable puppies. Mrs. Trainor must have
heard them stamping water from their shoes on
the mat in the foyer.

"I've been unhappy with myself all this day,"
she said gently, looking very frail and small under

the pile of snowy curls as she peered at them from the dark of her doorway. "I should have managed that errand myself instead of asking you to come back."

"It's no bother," Peter grinned, wiping the shiny raindrops off his freckles. "It's no day to play anything anyway, is it Greta?"

"We love having something to do," Greta answered.

"Then here's the key," Mrs. Trainor said, "since you insist on being so sweet. Do you know where my things are?"

Although there was a rickety handrail, the basement stairs seemed so narrow and dark even with the light on that it felt dangerous to Greta. When they reached the basement they passed a furnace, a big, hulking giant that seemed to slouch comfortably, waiting for winter.

Greta looked at the furnace almost fondly. She had always loved the winter furnace sounds all through the house. The steam rushing through the pipes set up such a busy, rackety clamor, she remembered. When the little valves on the ends of the heaters hissed noisily, it always seemed quite as cheery as a fireplace somehow. One of the radiators in the topmost story was near a window.

In the winter, Greta liked to curl up close to it with a book and warm herself so thoroughly that she must keep turning herself like a toasting bun to keep from feeling scorched. Just by glancing through the window, Greta could look out on the swaying descent of the snow. From up here it was clean and fresh-looking. It was like the near and far noises somehow. High snow and street snow were very different. Down on the walk it became clinging and dirty and was pushed about like a stray dog. But from the topmost window it was gracefully, cleanly free.

In the room behind the furnace stood a long row of storage lockers. There was a neat card lettered with the tenant's name on the front of each padlocked door: Knowles, for Peter's family, Miss Gray, Owens, McGraw, and all the others. The one marked Trainor was the largest. It was the first one they came to.

Peter fitted the key into the lock and turned it with a rough-boy jerk. As Greta watched, the lock sprang open at the key's touch, but surprisingly that was not all. A tiny length of the padlock loop fell tinkling to the concrete floor. Peter stared down at the broken lock in his hand.

"Did I do that?" he asked guiltily. He knew that he had been showing off a little.

"You couldn't have," Greta assured him, picking up the broken-off piece and looking at it closely. "It had already been sawed off where it fits into the lock."

"Somebody has been into this locker without a key, then," Peter commented logically.

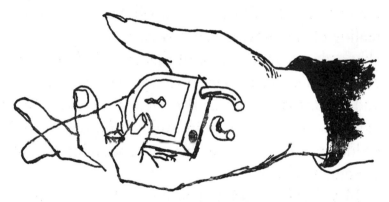

On a sudden impulse, Greta tugged at the other locks on down the line. Each of them slid from the door easily, all neatly sawed as Mrs. Trainor's had been.

"Don't touch anything," Peter ordered, sounding a little frightened. "You stay right here and watch while I bring Mrs. Trainor down." He was halfway up the narrow stairs when he glanced back at Greta watching him from behind the locker cabinets.

"You aren't scared, are you?" he asked as an afterthought.

"A little," Greta admitted honestly, almost whispering. "Just hurry up."

Although it was only minutes before Peter returned with Mrs. Trainor, somehow it was a frightening time. To Greta it seemed that the whole feeling of the gray, cavernous basement had been changed just by the clink of that sawed-off lock on the floor. The big furnace no longer seemed friendly and waiting but more as if it were crouching. The dark places under the stairs and behind the lockers suddenly seemed to be hiding places instead of sleeping shadows.

Mrs. Trainor came down the stairs carefully, favoring her injured foot, with Peter just behind her. A wrinkle of concern on her face showed that Peter must have told her what they had found.

"Peter must be wrong," she told Greta reassuringly as they approached. "That lock is rather old and must be broken off."

As she held the lock in her hand and studied it, her expression changed.

"Why would anyone do that?" she asked Peter, looking very distressed now.

"Maybe you should check inside and see if anything's missing," Greta suggested.

With Peter's nod of encouragement, Mrs. Trainor sighed unhappily and began piling things out on the floor and exploring the contents of her locker. While she did this, Greta watched Peter. His round freckled face was wrinkled with his thinking look. She wondered if he was remembering the bars of the ventilator and how neatly they had been sawed through in just this same way. Perhaps with the same saw, Greta reflected unhappily.

"This is very peculiar," Mrs. Trainor said when her examination was complete. "There's not a single thing missing that I can discover. Maybe it was just a prank." She said this hopefully as if she wished that they would agree with her.

"It's a very strange sort of prank," Peter commented quietly. "Maybe there's something gone from some of the others."

"Do you think I should call Officer Mullens?" she asked doubtfully.

"There isn't much he could do until the others come home," Greta pointed out. "Nobody would know what was missing except the people who use the lockers."

"Of course, you're right," Mrs. Trainor agreed quickly. "I'll notify everyone this evening, and then we'll have him come in if anything is missing.

"I almost forgot what we came for." She smiled suddenly as if everything had been settled just by deciding what was to be done. She fished in the back of the locker and drew a curtain rod from a bundle. "Here's one that will fit."

Peter put up the curtain rod for her, working more quickly than Greta had ever seen him do.

They left for upstairs with Mrs. Trainor's thanks still soft in their ears.

"There's a great deal about all this that I don't like," Peter said pompously, hurrying Greta up the stairs until he himself was panting from the effort of the climb.

"I feel as Mrs. Trainor does," Greta replied. "If there's nothing missing, why should the lockers be broken into, unless it's a prank?"

"Let's switch mysteries for a minute," Peter grinned at her. "I'm willing to wait and see if anything's gone. Right now I want to see old star-eyes in your closet."

Peter unlocked the door and hung the key carefully on its nail before going into the closet. Because of the moisture of the rainy day, the little door was stuck tighter than usual. Peter had to pull so hard that he fell all in a heap when it finally came free.

There was not enough room for both of their heads at the opening, so Greta waited back in the closet. But when Peter gave a long whistle of amazed surprise she could not stand it. Squatting by him on the floor, she stared through the opening too.

It was still there, the broad bulky garment like a man's coat, with the plumed hat above it. But now, where the face should have been, there were eyes, bright yellow eyes that blinked lazily at them before Caliph jumped in through the ventilator. He paraded tail-high through the little garret room with dusty spider webs catching in loops like Christmas tinsel in his rain-damp fur.

"Oh, Caliph," Greta sighed, her breath coming out hard around the little scared place that formed in her throat.

"Get me a light, Greta," Peter ordered with excited urgency.

Because it was quicker than going to the kitchen for a flashlight, Greta unhooked her bed lamp and handed it into the closet.

The cord of the lamp was just long enough to let the light into the garret space even though the lamp itself would not go in.

By this light Peter and Greta could see the "man in the closet" for what he really was. A bulky, broad-shouldered garment swayed a little from its hanger, which was suspended from a long line of wire that ran the length of the unfinished part of the garret. This line was almost solid with such hangers; a whole row of them lined up like poorly laundered ghosts in the cool of the dark garret. Above this row,

also running the length of the space, was a long
shelf completely filled with hats.

Greta thought she had never seen so many
clothes at once. She watched as Peter went in and
carefully pulled the cover from the one she had
mistaken for a man in the glow of her flashlight.

As Peter held the sheet-like cover in his hand,
Greta gasped, "How beautiful!"

"It sure is," Peter agreed, as they admired the
dark velvet gown, old-fashioned in style but still
richly beautiful, the fabric gleaming in the light

from Greta's little lamp. Deep folds of lace looped around the collar and the overskirt. The hat above matched it perfectly except for the blue plume that had escaped its covering. It had been faded and dust stained to a murky gray by exposure to the uncertain light of the little attic.

Going down the line, they unwrapped the hangers one by one and admired the clothes. There was even a lovely Grecian robe, all white except for a trimming of gold braid that had tarnished darkly through the years. Greta felt she would explode with excitement.

"Mrs. Trainor's stage clothes. They're unbelievable. Oh Peter, do you suppose she knows they're here?"

"It's hard to tell," Peter said thoughtfully. "I remember her telling you that she had saved them for a long time. It sounded as if she didn't have them anymore, the way she said that."

"Peter," Greta said suddenly. "Do you remember what Mrs. Trainor said the day she had that fall? When she was just coming to and wasn't very sensible, she kept repeating 'So bright, so beautiful, a star for a star.' She admitted she was looking for something. Is it possible that she could have meant these?"

Peter shook his head emphatically. "Not possibly, Greta," he told her firmly.

"But she said herself that there was a fortune in clothes."

Peter continued to shake his head. "She's kind of funny, the way she searches around all the time and thinks she hears hansom cabs out in the street, but she's not crazy. She knows that all these bulky clothes and big heavy hats couldn't be hidden away in drawers or in a cabinet up over a stove."

Greta sat on a cross beam, holding the hem of a full, black costume in her hand. "You're right," she agreed slowly. "We never seem to figure anything out really. We just keep piling one mystery on top of the other and not getting anyplace. What do we really know?"

Peter numbered the things on his chubby fingers. "That she's looking for something small. That it's bright and beautiful and for a star. And, Greta . . ." She looked up startled at the way his voice had dropped mysteriously. "By now we're sure that somebody else is looking for it, too."

It was so very silent in the garret for a moment that Caliph's purring cadence was the only sound.

"Do you suppose it's up here somewhere?" she asked slowly.

"Whoever else is looking seems to think so," Peter said glumly. "Or why would they have sawed through the ventilator bars to get a look inside?"

"I'll get that flashlight," Greta volunteered. "Maybe there is something up here besides clothes and hats."

Peter was poking about listlessly in a dark place when she returned. "We'll have to look very fast," she warned. "It's already five o'clock, and I don't want us to be here when Mother comes. Somehow it seems that this mystery should belong to you and me and Mrs. Trainor."

With the help of the flashlight, the search went on quickly. Back under the eaves they found two wooden chests. Peter lugged them out and since they were not locked Greta lifted the lid of the smaller one as Peter held the light.

A funny, familiar smell rose from the inside, reminding Greta of something she could not identify at once. Not until she lifted the tissue and found a spray of dried flowers tied with a wide yellow ribbon did she recognize the smell. In the parlor of the old family home in Vermont was a rose jar that smelled like this, only spicier.

Under the flowers they found letters. The script was pale, looking more drawn than written, with huge scrolls on the capitals, and the quaintest phrases. Greta read only the first few lines before she felt quite embarrassed. She slipped the letter back into its envelope, closing the flap with the broken piece of sealing wax still heavy on the sheer paper.

"These are very private souvenirs," she told Peter, closing the lid.

Peter was delving in the other chest already. "These are funny things for a lady to keep," he said thoughtfully.

"What are they?" Greta asked, staring at the faded clothes he was pulling from the chest.

"It's a soldier's uniform," Peter replied.

"With those pants?" Greta asked.

"They're from the First World War," Peter explained. "This was the way English soldiers dressed then."

"Mrs. Trainor's husband was a soldier and he was English," Greta said thoughtfully, folding the clothes carefully as Peter lifted them out. "She went over to Europe to entertain the troops and fell in love and married him in England. These must have been his things."

As Peter was silent, Greta leaned over to see what he was doing.

"From here on it's just envelopes full of papers, all marked by years." Greta reached for one and slipped out the yellowed newsprint carefully.

"Look how beautiful," she breathed, staring at the picture of Mrs. Trainor on the top clipping. "Star Morgan to Entertain Yanks." She read the headline wonderingly. "Why do they put it like that?" she asked Peter curiously. "Her name isn't Star?"

"Maybe because she was a star on the stage," Peter said.

"This is funny," Greta went on, still studying the clipping. "Underneath it says, 'Star wearing her famous trademark'. Do you see a star on her anywhere?"

Peter looked carefully, then shrugged. "Not that shows."

Greta turned thoughtfully through Mrs. Trainor's clippings. There was one that mentioned her star twinkling in the footlights. "Peter, somewhere there is a special star that she always wore. Could that be what she was talking about the day she was hurt? Do you suppose that's what she meant when she kept repeating, 'So bright, so beautiful, a star for a star'?"

"If it were a star-shaped diamond or something, maybe," Peter said. "But there's nothing in those pictures like that."

Greta looked carefully at them again. The clothes changed a little in style through the different envelopes. But Mrs. Trainor had rather a style of her own, Greta decided. Her costumes always showed a cinch-belted dress, very full, and above it a wide, plumed hat.

"You can't spend all day mooning over those," Peter said finally. "There are lots more here and it's getting late." He lifted the rest of the envelopes out and piled them on the floor.

"Oh, no," he said despairingly. "There are just more clothes here in the bottom."

"More clothes?" Greta asked curiously, peering into the chest.

"Gloves, purses, a belt, and this purple thing," Peter said tiredly.

"Oh, I know what that is," Greta exclaimed delightedly. "That must be the queen's dress, the one that was torn when the curtain fell and nearly caused an accident."

Peter was stacking the things back in rapidly. "I have to rush. Mom and Dad will be home any

minute now, and I have my work to do. We'll have
to give this place a thorough search tomorrow. IT,
whatever *it* is, just has to be here."

After Peter left for his own apartment downstairs, Greta went to her window. Although she was
no longer afraid of the garret behind the door, she
still did not want to be back in there alone.

Darkness was coming quickly. Watching from
the high window, she could see no sidewalk at all,
only the tops of bobbing umbrellas as people hurried to find the warmth of their own homes. When
one gay plaid umbrella broke from the parade and
turned toward the front of the Trainor house, Greta

ran to turn the heat on under the teakettle. Mother would be home as soon as she could mount the stairs to the topmost story.

But dinner was late for the whole Trainor house that night. Mrs. Trainor stopped all the tenants as they entered the hall. She caught them closing their umbrellas in little puddles and folding their coats inside-out to keep the moisture from their clothes. They were confused and a little puzzled as she asked all of them to check the contents of their lockers because of the damaged locks that had been found.

Greta kept very quiet as she went back downstairs to the basement with her mother. Some of the people were annoyed and suspicious and seemed almost unhappy when they could find nothing gone. They talked loudly about dinner being delayed and the inconvenience of the whole thing.

Miss Gray seemed the most upset. "There's nothing missing here," she said with relief. "But I think the police should know about this."

The murmuring discussion among the others seemed to confuse Mrs. Trainor. "I hate to start an investigation or anything," she said unhappily. "I could just have all new locks put on."

A large man from the second floor, whom Greta rarely saw, grunted unhappily. "There's likely to be no end to this mischief unless we at least report it to the neighborhood officer. That should keep the vandals from any more tricks."

Then Mr. Owens spoke up. Greta felt suddenly cold all over when she looked at him and saw the sneering smile he gave Peter and her. "It seems wasteful to take police time with obviously childish mischief," he said pointedly. "Who has time to fiddle and pry and poke around like this anyway?"

Greta felt her mother's arm slip about her comfortingly. With growing horror, Greta realized that Mrs. Trainor and Mother were staring at Peter and

her. Greta felt her eyes filling with tears. She had
thought that all these people were her friends. Even
Mrs. Trainor did not meet her eyes. Mrs. Trainor
was staring fixedly at Mr. Owens with a look of
wide-eyed amazement.

Everyone is blaming it on us, Greta thought
miserably.

Even Mother's arm tightening about her shoulder did not help. It was as if all the staring eyes were
saying, "Guilty, guilty, guilty."

Greta tore loose from her mother's arm with a
sob and ran upstairs crying bitterly.

⛫ ⛫ 6 ⛫ ⛫

Although Greta ran quickly, she could hear her mother's footsteps following not far behind. Throwing herself across the pink striped bedspread, Greta wept helplessly. She just could not stand it. All her friends, Miss Gray and the others—especially Mrs. Trainor—thinking that she and Peter had sawed their locks to poke and pry as that horrid Mr. Owens had said.

For the first time Greta agreed with her mother about the city. She wanted to run away, to Vermont, anywhere to escape those awful eyes crying, "Guilty, guilty," as plain as words.

"But darling," her mother said softly, sitting on

the bed and cradling Greta's head on her lap. "You and Peter mustn't mind him. That man just put the idea in everyone's head. They don't believe it, I'm sure."

"But it makes me feel horrid," Greta sobbed.

"You should never feel bad unless you've done something wrong," her mother said firmly. "If your conscience is free, you must hold your head high and not let . . ."

Greta sat up quickly, holding her head high but not in the way that her mother meant at all. She suddenly felt that she and Peter had been very wrong to keep the mysteries to themselves instead of telling Mrs. Trainor. "Mother, I . . ." Greta began.

Hearing a rap at the door, Greta's mother got up and smoothed her skirt. Going to answer it, she smiled back at Greta reassuringly. "I'll be right back, honey," she said.

It was Peter. But it wasn't cocksure Peter with the eager, grinning face this time. He looked downcast as he came in quietly.

"I told my folks all about the garret, Greta," he blurted out when he was scarcely inside the door. "They said we must go straight to Mrs. Trainor and tell her everything."

"Garret?" Greta's mother asked in confusion.

"Of course, that's right," Greta sighed. "I was just about to tell Mother, too." She wiped her face again even though she knew it only made the tear streaks worse. "But I'm sure a crybaby."

"I'm terribly in the dark," Greta's mother said. "What garret? Greta, you haven't . . . ?" Her look was almost fearful.

"We didn't do anything wrong, Mother, I promise you." Greta took her mother's hand reassuringly. "We'll tell both you and Mrs. Trainor right now."

The rain had made the air so damp and chilly that Greta shivered a little as she and Peter waited in the hall for Mother to lock the door behind them. The tight, worried look on Mother's face made Greta feel terrible, but the sooner they got it over with, the better it would be.

Miss Gray was peering around the hall when they passed her floor. She looked at them fretfully, asking, "Have you seen my Caliph anywhere?"

"Not since about five," Peter told her.

"He's probably hiding somewhere," Miss Gray fussed. "He does so hate to be wet that he'll slip in wherever he can."

Greta kept trying to remember what Mother had

said about holding your head high when you had
not done anything wrong. But as they neared Mrs.
Trainor's apartment, she felt funny and wiggly-
nervous inside.

Mrs. Trainor greeted them with a happy cry.
Leaning over, she kissed Greta quickly and patted
Peter cordially on the shoulder.

"I'm so glad you're here," she said in her rich,
soft voice. "I was going to make that long trip upstairs to talk to both of you. Nobody really believes
that you did that silly thing to the lockers. You are
both too sensible to do a thing like that. Still, I
didn't want you to worry. It's a dreadful feeling
when people doubt your word."

"You're very sweet, Mrs. Trainor," Greta's
mother said, accepting the blue velvet chair that
Mrs. Trainor offered. "But it seems that the children have something they want to tell you."

"It's been such a full day," Mrs. Trainor sighed,
sitting erect and graceful on the love seat. "Such
peculiar things . . ." Her voice trailed off strangely.
"Did I ever tell you about Johnny Olliphant?" she
asked Greta brightly. "Such a talented young playwright! He dined here often with the cast in the
old days. And just today it seemed . . ."

Oh dear, Greta thought miserably, she is going

to go dancing off into the past again and make it ever so hard to explain the garret.

But Mrs. Trainor stopped, drawing a slender hand across her eyes. "It must have been that fall I had," she explained apologetically. "I had this same feeling the other day." Her voice was firmer now and bright. "Now, what did you sweet children want to talk to me about?"

Peter looked at Greta so appealingly that she had to begin.

"There was a noise behind my wall one night," she began quickly. "And when I went to look, I found a door in my closet."

"I think," Mrs. Trainor said gently, as Greta paused, "I think there are doors in all the closets, dear."

"A little door," Greta went on hastily, "way in the back, all papered over. And when I opened it, Miss Gray's cat Caliph jumped out."

It troubled Greta even more to see that both Mrs. Trainor and her mother were making little "O's" of confusion with their mouths.

"I thought there was a man in there with a star for a face, but it was really just the bars of the ventilator sawed through to let the sky show and your clothes, from the plays." Greta tumbled it all out in a breathless rush.

"Oh dear." Mrs. Trainor shook her white curls. "I must not be listening right." Then she smiled brightly. "My clothes? My stage clothes? How wonderful. I thought I had lost them, too."

"There are other things there, too," Greta went on eagerly. "Peter and I were looking just this afternoon."

"This is in your closet?" Mother asked strangely.

"That's entirely reasonable," Mrs. Trainor said. "I was away when the house was done over. You see," her voice dropped sadly, "my husband was never well after the war was over. I retired from the stage to travel with him in the hope that he might regain his strength. But our luck had run out, I guess. It was while we were away that my sisters made our house into these apartments. Where you live used to be the garret where I stored things over the years."

"Wouldn't you like to come and see the things?" Greta asked hopefully.

"And have a bite of supper with us," Greta's mother urged, regaining her poise a little. "We would all do better with some hot food, I'm sure."

"That sounds charming," Mrs. Trainor agreed. Her eyes sparkled happily. "I'm so excited about your discovery." When she returned from getting her door key and a pale gray stole which she pulled about her shoulders, she smiled at Greta wistfully. "There's something I have been looking for. Perhaps I will find it there." She said it as if her search were a secret, just between them.

Now that the story was told, Greta no longer felt tight and funny in her stomach. She traded a quick grin with Peter. It was so strange that Mrs. Trainor did not realize that everyone knew she was looking for something. Greta was sorry that Mrs. Trainor was not going to find it among the things in the garret, because she looked so gay and confident. Whatever it was that was "bright and beautiful" and "a star for a star" was not among what Greta and Peter had found.

After Mother unlocked the door and before she found the light switch, Greta had a peculiar feeling that she had walked into a cave. It was windy in the apartment and much colder than the hall outside. When the light flooded the room, Greta's mother gave a shriek of reproof. "Greta," she cried aghast. "Your window is open and it's raining in!"

"It can't be," Greta wailed, following her mother into the bedroom. "I shut it and locked it myself."

They all stared dumbly at the mess in Greta's room. The window pane was broken, and water ran in uneven little streams along the boards of the floor. The usually crisp white curtains hung limply drenched, stained with black where they had blown in and out over the fire escape rail outside.

"Has it been hailing?" Mrs. Trainor asked innocently. "Rain doesn't break a window like that very often."

"Peter," Greta's mother said briskly, still staring at the pieces of glass littering the floor. "You go and call Officer Mullens. I saw him pass the Chinese laundry when we came through the hall. Tell him to come quickly."

While Peter was gone, Greta's mother insisted that Mrs. Trainor sit in the tiny kitchen to eat a piece of toast with her tea. "The way this evening is going," Mother explained grimly, "it looks as if it will be forever until supper."

When Peter returned with Officer Mullens, she had hot cocoa and sandwiches ready for the children. Even Peter was finally warmed up by the time

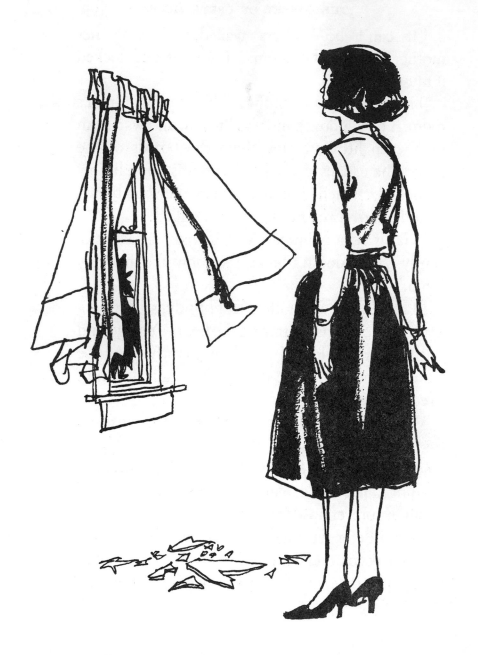

they had brought the policeman up-to-date on all that had happened.

"I want to get this clear. The ventilator bars were sawed through, the lockers downstairs were broken into but nothing was missing, and now this window looks as if it had been deliberately broken out." Officer Mullens recounted this slowly.

Greta and Peter nodded.

"Then the next thing is to see if anything is missing from that garret," the policeman said calmly, pressing broad hands flat on the table to rise.

The big beam of the police flashlight moved swiftly about the enclosure. Since Officer Mullen's wide bulk filled the opening, Greta waited with Peter until the policeman backed out, still bent from the pitch of the roof.

"A long row of clothes hangers, no telling what's missing from there, a shelfful of hats, and a wooden chest. Is that right?" he asked.

"Two wooden chests," Greta corrected quickly.

He looked at her sharply before disappearing within. He returned, carrying the smaller of the two chests which she and Peter had examined earlier. "This is the only one in there," he stated positively.

Mrs. Trainor grinned almost girlishly and then

blushed very pink when she lifted the lid. She shut it again at once, saying softly, "I remember this one; there's nothing of importance in this at all."

"The other one had newspapers in it," Peter said. "And some folded clothes and stuff in the bottom."

"I saved all the clippings," Mrs. Trainor interrupted. "I had quite forgotten that."

Officer Mullens went to the telephone, and they sat nervously listening to him order a guard to be put on the doors and at the fire escape. "We'll search this entire house first," he said matter-of-factly. "The first people to suspect would be the ones living here."

"But the chest was valuable only to me," Mrs. Trainor protested worriedly.

Almost everyone submitted quite genially to the search. They had finished their dinners now and even looked quite cordially at Peter and Greta waiting out in the hall as each apartment was examined.

Officer Mullens had a set of questions he asked before exploring the rooms. "Have you been outside since returning from work?" he asked first. No one had, until they reached Miss Gray's apartment. With her, the question was hardly necessary. Her hair was dewy with rain, and the coat laid across the straight chair inside the door was dripping a dark circle on the newspaper folded neatly beneath it.

"Several times," she told Officer Mullens shortly. "I can't find Caliph."

"Her cat," Peter explained in a whisper to the policeman, who looked a little confused. Greta almost giggled. How was Officer Mullens to know that Caliph was the name of Miss Gray's Persian cat.

"I saw him on the fire escape while I fixed our dinner," she went on fretfully. "Then, when it was ready, he had disappeared."

"We'll keep an eye out for him," the policeman promised with a smile as they left her apartment.

At the Owens apartment Peter and Greta held back. Greta did not want to see that man again. She agreed with Mother that he had started the suspicion against herself and Peter. Greta felt she never wanted to see his face again because of that.

"Go out?" Mr. Owens boomed in a hearty voice at the policeman's question. "On a night like this?" Greta realized that he had not really answered, and she hoped that Officer Mullens would notice the dripping raincoat over the chair in the kitchen beyond.

Peter saw Caliph first. He punched Greta hard

and pointed. Mrs. Trainor was staring at Mr.
Owens with that peculiar searching look, but what
Peter meant was a long yellow tail looped from
behind the back of the divan in the corner.

"Kitty, kitty, kitty," Greta called softly. She was
depending on the saucers of milk she had fed
Caliph to lure him out. It worked.

He walked regally out from behind the divan, his
plume of a tail high and his broad whiskered face
tilted hungrily at her.

Mr. and Mrs. Owens were as surprised as anyone.
"How did that cat get in here?" Mrs. Owens asked
sharply.

"He was out on the fire escape a few minutes
ago," Greta said pointedly. Her hint seemed to
work. Officer Mullens stuck his head in the door to
look at the Owens's bedroom window which
opened right onto the dripping fire escape.

Looking at Mrs. Owens brought all sorts of
things back to Greta in a tumble of remembering;
the curious way she had stared into Greta's apartment, the woman's anger when the children had
surprised her drawing the house. Then there was
that discussion with Mother about swapping apartments. And that very first day, Greta recalled with
sudden excitement, why, Mrs. Owens herself had

asked about the garret before Greta even found it.

As Officer Mullens attempted to examine the Owens's rooms, as he had all the others, Mr. Owens began arguing about a legal paper of some kind. Mrs. Owens's doll-like face was tense and white as she listened to them.

Suddenly Mrs. Trainor's voice broke in, interrupting as if she had not heard a word that anyone was saying. "John Olliphant," she said in delighted surprise. "Just the same after so long!"

Mr. Owens jumped at her words, and Greta saw his hand start to tremble on the doorknob. But Mrs. Owens began to sob, finally burying her face in her hands and crying helplessly, as Greta herself had done in the basement just an hour or so before.

"It's no use, George," she said brokenly. "It's no use at all if she recognizes you."

Officer Mullens looked at both of them silently. Mr. Owens, his face twitching unhappily as he looked at his sobbing wife, said, "Maybe you had better come in and talk."

Mr. Owens looked smaller somehow as he sat by his wife on the divan. "She's right about my name being Olliphant," he said slowly, "but it's George, not John. John was my father."

"Who was this John Olliphant?" Officer Mullens asked. "And why are you going under a false name here?"

"Johnny was just the best young playwright in America when I was on the stage," Mrs. Trainor said defensively. "Mr. Owens looks just like him."

"If your father was so great," Officer Mullens asked pointedly, "why are you here under an assumed name?"

Mr. Owens seemed to be struggling for an answer. Officer Mullens went on. "With all that rain on the floor under your window and that cat in here, I shall search this apartment for certain. Do you want to cooperate, or shall I have a warrant issued?"

"You might as well go ahead," Mr. Owens said calmly. "There's a chest of newspaper clippings here that doesn't belong to me."

Greta was completely astonished. It did not seem believable that Mr. Owens should submit so easily after the way he had acted.

"What about the damage done to the basement storage locker? Did you have a hand in that, too?" Officer Mullens paused only a minute. "We have fingerprints from all those locks."

"I did it," Mr. Owens said very contritely. Suddenly he began to talk very fast as if it were important for him to convince everyone. "You see, I was planning a book about my father's career. There was some information I couldn't locate." As he talked, Greta watched his eyes move very swiftly between Officer Mullens and Mrs. Trainor as if he were trying to convince them with his straight looks. "I was sure that what I needed would be here somewhere."

"Why didn't you just ask me for it?" Mrs. Trainor asked. "I would have been glad to help."

Mrs. Trainor looked shocked and hurt as the man addressed his answer to Officer Mullens. "I had understood that Mrs. Trainor had grown a little . . . eccentric. I thought it would be easier this way."

Officer Mullens made no reply, but his face puffed a little. Greta was glad to see his expression change. Mr. Owens did not realize how fond everyone was of Mrs. Trainor or he never would have said that.

"I don't know what that word 'ec—, ec—' something or other means," Peter interrupted angrily. "But I don't like your saying it."

Mr. Owens was suddenly so contrite and so co-operative that Greta was almost frightened. It did not make sense for anyone to change so rapidly. "Bring Mrs. Trainor's chest, my dear." He spoke to his wife so sweetly that Greta almost snorted. "And I owe you children an apology, too," he went on in the same oily way. "We were wrong to try to cast the blame on you about the lockers. But we were getting so close that we didn't want to take the chance of a police investigation keeping us from finding the clippings."

Peter did not acknowledge the apology. He only stared coldly at Mr. Owens.

"We were wrong to do it like this," Mrs. Owens said, in the same insincere way in which her husband had been speaking. She smiled a careful smile as she set the chest before Mrs. Trainor.

"I hope you'll forgive us for what we did," Mrs. Owens said meekly. "We do need the clippings from this chest so much for the book."

Greta met a disturbed look from Peter. He was afraid of the same thing she was—that this smiling, apologetic pair would fool the policeman and Mrs. Trainor.

"Regardless of your motive," Officer Mullens interrupted, "you have been guilty of breaking and entering and destroying private property." He wrote very quickly in his little book while Mrs. Trainor knelt excitedly and opened the chest.

"Why did you choose tonight?" Officer Mullens

asked, eyeing the Owenses coldly. At least Greta hoped she was right about his expression.

"When that little fat boy (Peter looked pained at the words) went tearing upstairs and then they all came down together, I figured something had been found and I'd better hurry. While they were all downstairs, I broke the window and got the clippings," the man replied.

Mrs. Owens was watching Mrs. Trainor with that smile that stopped before it reached her eyes. As Mrs. Trainor lifted the uniform from the chest, her eyes grew very misty and she drew it to her with a sad little breath that made Greta hurt inside. It suddenly became very quiet in the room, as Officer Mullens and Mrs. Trainor emptied the contents of the chest on the floor.

"My purple gown," Mrs. Trainor said in surprise, as they neared the bottom of the chest. "My sisters must have used this chest for all sorts of odds and ends."

"You mean you don't know what was originally in here?" Officer Mullens asked in dismay.

"These things were all stored while I was traveling with my sick husband," she explained gently. "But here are the clippings they wanted."

Peter was biting his lip in a strange, thoughtful

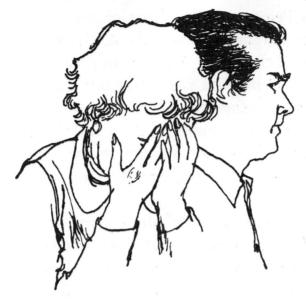

way. Greta was sure that the look that Mr. and Mrs. Owens exchanged was one of relief.

"We're so sorry that we didn't come right to you . . ." Mr. Owens started. Suddenly Peter's voice broke in, and Officer Mullens looked at him sharply.

"Uniforms, clippings, purple dress, purses . . . belt. There's a fancy belt missing." He said it triumphantly as if he had struggled to remember what was missing from the pile of things on the floor.

"Belt?" Mrs. Trainor asked eagerly, suddenly excited. "What kind of belt, Peter?"

As Peter made the shape of the belt with his hands and started to describe it, Greta saw the expression change on Mr. Owens's face. He glared fiercely at his wife as she began to cry again in a funny, frightened way.

"Wide in the middle," Peter said slowly, "then narrow on both ends and with some stones set in."

"Stones," Mrs. Trainor said excitedly. "Are you sure, Peter?"

"But there was no belt in this chest," Mr. Owens said firmly, although his face had turned very white.

"There was. It must have been. I have looked every other place, again and again." Mrs. Trainor smiled gently. "So bright, so beautiful, a star for a star."

"Do we need the search warrant?" Officer Mullens asked quietly, as Mr. Owens stirred uncomfortably under his glance.

There was only a moment of silence before Mrs. Owens rose and, in spite of her husband's quick clutch at her arm, left the room. In a moment she was back, carrying the belt Peter had described. She handed it to Mrs. Trainor silently. Her face was not pretending to smile now; it was cold with defeat and puffy from crying.

Peter and Greta leaned forward eagerly as the

belt was spread out. It was a lovely thing, large enough only for the daintiest waist. Made of soft white leather, it was set with stones as Peter had said. But here in the light from the lamp the stones looked different, as Peter admitted later. There was a circle of small red stones, and in the middle a huge blue jewel that winked at them from its heart like the first star of evening in a dark sky.

"A star sapphire," Greta's mother breathed in wonder. "And so big!"

Mrs. Trainor smiled, looking very pleased. "My lucky star. It was a gift from the prince," she explained to Peter. "Every time I wore this stone I had good luck. I never went on stage without it after I discovered this. I had it stitched in a belt so I could wear it always. He called it a star for a star, and it brought me fame and fortune." Even as she said this, her eyes grew sad.

"But how did it come to be put away and lost?" Greta asked.

"When my husband became ill, it seemed that its luck was spent. The last time we visited in America, I left it here as I no longer believed in it."

"It sure wasn't lucky for this pair," the policeman grumbled, as he went to the door to call another officer to take the Owenses away.

"It will be lucky for me again," Mrs. Trainor said brightly. "That's why I looked for it so hard. Now that I've found it, I can sell it and use the money to get my house fixed. My lucky star will save the home I love." She smiled at Peter and Greta very happily as she explained this.

"I think it's these kids that bring you luck," Officer Mullens said, happy now that Mr. and Mrs. Owens were gone. "First that fall on the gas jet when they saved your life, and now this. You owe them everything."

"And I'm going to reward them," Mrs. Trainor said happily. "For saving my home, what would you like most in the whole wide world?"

She turned to Peter and Greta as she asked this, and the lights in her eyes were not less bright than the star sapphire in her hand.

"What would you like the most in the whole world?" Greta repeated to herself. She stared at Mrs. Trainor, her eyes wide with wonder. These were the very same words that she and Peter used when they played the going-home game called "Wish." They usually wished for ponies to ride or a bicycle or a trip in a boat. Peter always said he would go to Ireland because they would not make remarks about his freckles there.

But now that the wish was real, Greta found that what she wanted the most was not any of these.

Her words came out almost breathlessly because she meant them so sincerely.

"I'd like to live in the topmost story all my life until I'm grown up," she said solemnly. "With everything just as it is now."

Then Greta noticed her mother's face, and the happiness turned to hurt. Oh, why hadn't she thought? She ran to her mother and hugged her tight, saying, "I'm sorry, Mother. I shouldn't have said that at all. I forgot about your wanting to move back to Vermont and live in the country. That's what I really, truly want because it will make you happy."

Because Greta's arms were holding her tight, the words came funny and squeezed from her mother, who was doing something that was not laughing or crying, but something in-between. "Why, Greta-pet, I only wanted to live in Vermont for your sake. I never realized how much your friends here mean to you, and there's more than enough excitement to keep me happy here." She winked at Officer Mullens. "Here I've been waiting to make you happy and you were happy already. I think your wish is wonderful."

Peter grinned when Mrs. Trainor turned the question to him. "I guess I'm as silly as Greta," he said embarrassed. "I'd just like to stay here and get grown-up and maybe go to Police School later." He added this last shyly with a little grin at Officer Mullens.

When it was all over, Officer Mullens took the jewels to the precinct house for safekeeping overnight. Caliph curled up clean and dry under a footstool in Miss Gray's bedroom. Everyone had rejoiced at Mrs. Trainor's good luck, and finally Greta and her mother were climbing the stairs to the topmost story.

The rain was falling more gently now. It did not sweep into the room but dripped down in straight lines between the tall buildings. Greta and her mother looked through the broken window, listening to the far noises: muted horns and the splash of wheels in the wet streets below. Greta knew how scattered rainbows would be forming in the puddles there, city rainbows made of oil washed from the busy street. The pigeons complained softly from the opposite ledge, and the sidewalks below gleamed under the street light.

"I guess it *is* pretty wonderful," Greta's mother said softly. "And it's home."

After they patched the broken pane by fitting
the side of a big oatmeal carton into the space,
Greta went sound asleep listening to the chuckle of
the rain flowing down the gutters outside.

ABOUT THE AUTHOR

Born in Kansas, *Mary Francis Shura* has spent most of her life in Missouri. She is a widow and the mother of three children who range in age from fifteen to four years old.

The Shura family live on "Shura 'Nuff Farm" which has a frog-full pond, a little grove, five acres of grass and a regal cottonwood in the dooryard.

When starting *The Garret of Greta McGraw* the author says that she "tried to bring back the excited pleasure and the lively memories of a childhood spent in a booming city."

Mrs. Shura is currently employed by the Kansas City Area Council of Girl Scouts as Community Relations Director.

A NOTE ON THE TYPE

The text of this book was set on the Linotype in ELECTRA, designed by W. A. DWIGGINS. The Electra face is a simple and readable type suitable for printing books by present-day processes. It is not based on any historical model, and hence does not echo any particular time or fashion. It is without eccentricities to catch the eye and interfere with reading—in general, its aim is to perform the function of a good book printing-type: to be read, and not seen.

DATE DUE

DATE DUE		
FEB 1		
APR 14		
APR 28		
JAN 25		
FEB 9		
FEB 16		
NOV 2 1/7		